KIDS CAN'T STOP READING THE *CHOOSE YOUR OWN ADVENTURE®* STORIES!

"I like CHOOSE YOUR OWN ADVENTURE books because they're full of surprises. I can't wait to read more."

—Cary Romanos, age 12

"Makes you think thoroughly before making decisions."

—Hassan Stevenson, age 11

"I read five different stories in one night and that's a record for me. The different endings are fun."

—Timmy Sullivan, age 9

"It's great fun! I like the idea of making my own decisions."

—Anthony Ziccardi, age 11

And teachers like this series, too:

"We have read and reread, worn thin, loved, loaned, bought for others, and donated to school libraries our *Choose Your Own Adventure* books."

CHOOSE YOUR OWN ADVENTURE®— AND MAKE READING MORE FUN!

Bantam Books in the Choose Your Own Adventure® Series
Ask your bookseller for the books you have missed.

Choose Your Own Adventure Books for younger readers

CHOOSE YOUR OWN ADVENTURE® · 16

SURVIVAL AT SEA

BY EDWARD PACKARD

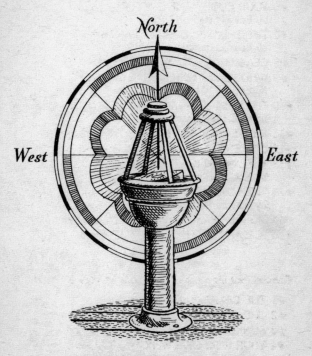

ILLUSTRATED BY PAUL GRANGER

BANTAM BOOKS
TORONTO · NEW YORK · LONDON · SYDNEY

RL 4, IL age 10 and up

SURVIVAL AT SEA

A Bantam Book / December 1982

*CHOOSE YOUR OWN ADVENTURE® is a registered
trademark of Bantam Books, Inc.
Original Conception of Edward Packard*

Illustrated by Paul Granger

ISBN 0-553-22768-8

Published simultaneously in the United States and Canada

Bantam Books are published by Bantam Books, Inc. Its trademark, consisting of the words "Bantam Books" and the por-
trayal of a rooster, is Registered in U.S. Patent and Trademark
Office and in other countries. Marca Registrada. Bantam
Books, Inc., 666 Fifth Avenue, New York, New York 10103.

PRINTED IN THE UNITED STATES OF AMERICA

O   0 9 8 7 6 5 4 3

To Connie,
with appreciation

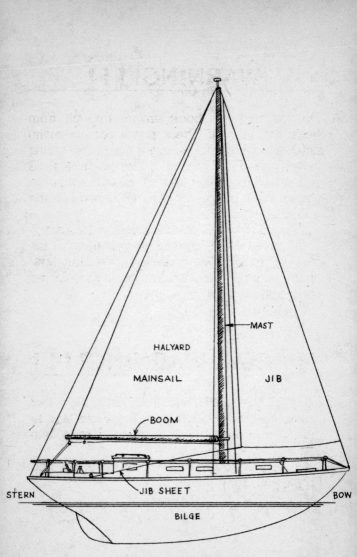

SLOOP *ALLEGRO*

WARNING! ! ! !

Do not read this book straight through from beginning to end! These pages contain many different adventures you might have while sailing in the South Pacific Ocean. From time to time as you read along, you will be asked to make a choice. What happens to you will depend on the decisions *you* make.

After you make each choice, follow the instructions to see what happens to you next. Think carefully before you make each decision. The ocean can yield untold riches, but it can also be very dangerous.

Good luck!

SPECIAL WARNING! ! ! !

On page 13, you'll find the ocean chart that shows where the *Allegro* is sailing. From time to time, you may need to look at the chart to help you make your decision.

I hope you survive your adventures at sea, and I hope you enjoy them!

- Edward Packard

A few weeks ago you got a call from your old friend, Dr. Nera Vivaldi, the famous anthropologist who specializes in interspecies communication.

"How would you like to go sailing in the South Pacific?" she asks. "We'll be searching for the Arkasaur, a dinosaur that we believe may still live in the ocean depths."

It took some arguing to get permission to go, but here you are on Bariba Island, thousands of miles from home. When the forty-foot sloop *Allegro* leaves Bariba harbor tomorrow, you'll be on board!

Right now, you are seated in front of the TV set in the lounge of the Bariba Hotel. With you are your crewmates: Eric Zindel, the *Allegro*'s skipper; Pete Karn, his young nephew; Jack Maiko, the deckhand; and, of course, Dr. Vivaldi.

You've tuned in to an interview with the captain of an Australian fishing trawler, a man who claims to have seen a huge aquatic beast in the area. You watch with keen interest as he describes what he saw:

> *We were about 400 miles northwest of Bariba when we sighted a black shape in the water. At first we thought it was a whale. But a long, thin neck and monstrous head rose up nearly thirty feet in the air. Its jaws must have been ten feet long.*

Turn to page 2.

2

We had men with harpoon guns ready to fire, but they didn't have a chance. The monster swung round a great orange flipper and swept them into the sea the way you'd knock a fly off a table.

I ordered the ship right full rudder, engines full speed, to get clear of the beast. We circled round to get another look, but it was gone.

A commercial comes on the screen, and Eric flicks off the set. "Well, Nera, what do you think?" he asks.

Dr. Vivaldi is already on her feet, her eyes flashing. "This may be a hoax, of course, but the description matches the Arkasaur perfectly. It could be the *one* species of dinosaur that still exists. This encounter took place in an area where a warm current, rich in nutrients, rises from the ocean floor. If the Arkasaur still lives, that's the only place we can expect to find it."

Go on to the next page.

Two days have passed. You're aboard the *Allegro*, sailing in a fair breeze under sunny skies. Eric is at the helm. Dr. Vivaldi stands nearby, analyzing a water sample. Pete is tending the jib, and Maiko is sitting on the foredeck staring out at the sea. You are about to check the depth finder when a message comes over the marine radio.

Turn to page 4.

Warning! A volcano has erupted just under the surface of the sea, about 200 miles east of Etuk Island. A new island is rising from the sea. All vessels are warned to keep clear of the area. There may be turbulent seas and tidal waves.

Turn to page 6.

6

Eric glances at the chart. "We're heading directly into the danger zone," he says. "I'm willing to go on, but only if everyone agrees. This may be our one chance to find the Arkasaur. But, if you don't want to risk the dangerous waters, say so now."

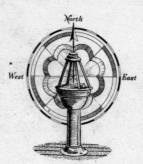

If you say you don't want to risk sailing into the danger zone, turn to page 18.

If you say that you're willing to risk it, turn to page 19.

"I would steer due north," you tell Dr. Vivaldi. "According to the chart, that's the course most likely to bring us to the area of the Arkasaur sightings."

Dr. Vivaldi turns the wheel. After trimming the sails for the new course, you and Pete sit on the foredeck, leaning up against the cabin, sipping lemonade and eating chocolate cookies, as you watch the sun slip into the sea. You climb into your bunk with the feeling that all is going well. As you drift into a peaceful sleep, you have a hunch that tomorrow you might sight the Arkasaur.

You are awakened by Maiko's cry. *"Breakers ahead!"* You crash into Dr. Vivaldi as you scramble up the ladder. Maiko is at the wheel. You hear Eric yelling from the bow. *"There are reefs all over the place! Bring 'er around!"*

You leap into the cockpit and loosen the jib. Maiko turns the wheel hard over. A wave catches the stern, sending the *Allegro* plummeting into its trough. There is a terrible crunching sound. You are thrown violently forward as the *Allegro* smashes into a reef.

"Quick, back the jib! See if we can get her off the reef!" Eric shouts.

You reach for the jib, but again you are thrown off balance as another wave knocks the *Allegro* on its side.

Turn to page 9.

"Too late," says Eric. "We're wedged in."

"We're taking on water!" cries Dr. Vivaldi. "The coral is cutting us to shreds."

Turn to page 10.

You look into the cabin. Water is gushing up from the bilge.

"Get the life raft!" Eric yells.

Maiko and Pete go for the raft. You hurry to get water and food, but Eric's cry stops you. *"Abandon ship!"* You help launch the raft, and the five of you pile in.

You and your crewmates paddle toward smoother water. Looking back, you watch wave after wave smash into the *Allegro*, slowly breaking it up against the sharp coral reef.

Soon the life raft is clear of the dangerous reefs. No one has much to say, as you drift helplessly on the ocean swells. You keep thinking about how you set the course straight for the reefs. If only you'd taken more time to look at the chart. Next time you'll know better—if there is a next time.

The End

Using every bit of your strength (and some you didn't even know you had) you try to turn the wheel slowly to the left. It won't budge. Then, suddenly, the wheel starts to spin, and you struggle to keep on course. But the wheel is slowing turning against you.

Looking back, you see a crest about to break behind you. You turn the wheel, steering more sharply across the mountainous wave, threading your way through the whitewater.

The great wave has passed. The boat rolls and pitches in the lumpy swells. You fall down, exhausted.

Dr. Vivaldi takes the wheel. "You saved the boat!" she says. The rest of the crew echoes her praise, except poor Eric, who is slumped over near the wheel, still dazed from the blow on the head.

Pete kneels beside his uncle and helps him up. "We must set her back on course," Eric says.

"A volcanic eruption is usually followed by aftershocks," Dr. Vivaldi warns. "The next one might finish us off. On the other hand, these disturbances might bring the Arkasaur to the surface." She hands you the chart. "What course shall I steer?" she asks.

Turn to page 12.

You study the chart. You know that you passed Kitt's Reef at the same time yesterday. You calculate that the *Allegro* has been heading northwest and traveling at about seven knots. The radio reported that the volcanic eruption took place about 200 miles east of Etuk Island. Which way will you tell Dr. Vivaldi to steer?

North?
Northeast?
East?
Southeast?
South?
Southwest?
West?
Northwest?

You may wish to check the chart (page 13) before making your decision. Then turn to page 27.

CAUTION: Do not turn to page 27 until you have firmly decided which way to tell Dr. Vivaldi to steer.

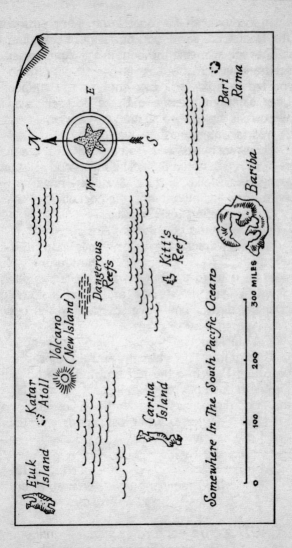

Etuk Island

Katar Atoll

Volcano (New Island)

Dangerous Reefs

Carina Island

Kitt's Reef

N E W S

Baribа

Bari Rama

Somewhere In The South Pacific Ocean

0   100   200   300 MILES

14

Trying to keep the boat from plunging down the face of the wave, you put all your strength to the wheel, swinging the boat to the right, parallel to the wave.

"Try to hold 'er!" Eric shouts. You snap on your safety harness and brace yourself as the wave rolls the *Allegro* all the way over on its side. A wall of water smashes over you.

The wave has passed. You are still alive, but the *Allegro* is a battered hulk. The masts and sails are gone. Eric, Maiko, and Dr. Vivaldi are nowhere in sight. Pete lies moaning in the cockpit.

"Are the others lost?" he asks.

You sadly nod your head. "Are you OK?"

"I think I cracked a rib," he says. "But forget about that. You'd better inflate the life raft." He gestures toward the bow of the boat. It is tilted down beneath the surface, and water is sloshing over the deck. "The wave smashed in the bow. We're going down."

You quickly inflate the raft. Taking only enough time to grab a tin of biscuits and a jug of water, you help Pete into the raft and jump in behind him. You push off from the *Allegro.* Seconds later the sloop disappears beneath the waves. You and Pete say a prayer for your lost friends, and then one for yourselves.

Turn to page 28.

You grab the wheel and hang on for your life! The boom swings wildly. It hits Eric on the head and knocks him down to the floor of the cockpit. Pete is thrown hard against the deck. Fortunately, Maiko has braced himself in the forward hatch.

At last, the *Allegro* levels off on the crest of the wave. You can look down at water for miles in all directions, as if you were looking down from the top of a mountain.

Then the boat tilts and starts to plunge down the side of the monster wave, surfing faster and faster. You now have a firm grip on the wheel. Which way should you try to steer?

If you keep the wheel where it is so that you continue straight down the wave, turn to page 21.

If you try to steer at a 45-degree angle to the wave, turn to page 11.

If you try to steer parallel to the wave, turn to page 14.

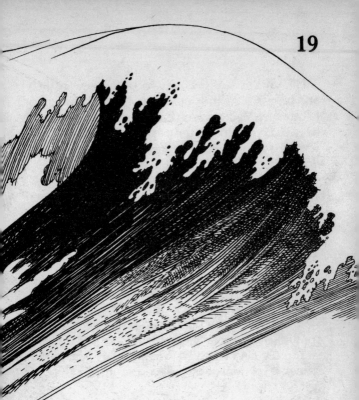

Suddenly you see that it makes no difference what you decide to do. A tremendous wave—fifty feet high—is about to hit the *Allegro*.

"Tie on your lifelines!" Eric yells. Before he can heed his own warning, though, he is thrown violently to the deck. The boat is almost set on end by a mountain of foaming blue-green water.

Turn to page 17.

Dr. Vivaldi sets the *Allegro* on its new course and turns the helm over to you. Eric still has a bad headache. Maiko keeps babbling about how rich he will be when he gets to the new island. Dr. Vivaldi seems a little depressed. "I've begun to doubt that we'll ever find the Arkasaur," she says.

But what has you most upset is the weather. The sky has filled with oily gray clouds. Whenever the sun breaks through, it shines with a sickly yellow light. The wind blows harder. Long deep swells roll toward you from the north, pitching the *Allegro* about. You check the barometer. It's falling rapidly.

As the afternoon passes, the wind picks up and the sea grows rough. Soon waves are breaking over the bow of the boat, sending sheets of heavy spray flying in your face.

You are glad when Dr. Vivaldi takes over at the wheel. "Tell Maiko to relieve me in a couple of hours," she says.

Turn to page 32.

Holding the wheel tightly, you keep the *Allegro* on course, straight down the face of the wave. Sheets of white spray fly over the deck, filling the air. The boat plunges as if it had plummeted over a cliff.

Then, through the spray, you see a wall of water rising ahead of you. Another wave breaks from behind. Tons of water crash over you as the *Allegro* plunges down, down, into the depths of the sea.

The End

Once Dr. Vivaldi has set the *Allegro* on its new course, you go below to sleep.

You're awakened early the next morning by excited voices above you. Eric is already climbing the ladder. You follow right behind.

The other crew members are on deck already. Everyone is looking out at a ring of cone-shaped peaks rising from the sea.

"What a beautiful island!" cries Dr. Vivaldi.

"Yes, I've been here before," says Eric. "It's Carina Island. It's a true paradise, but nowhere near where the Arkasaur was sighted." He looks at you sternly. "You set us on the wrong course. I don't believe you read the chart!"

You start to apologize, but Eric holds up a hand. "That's all right. You've given me a thought. We've survived a tidal wave, and I'm still shaky from that bang on the head. We will cruise to Carina Island. We all need a rest, so we'll spend a day or two swimming and sunbathing before we continue our search for the Arkasaur. Would that be all right with you, Dr. Vivaldi?" he asks.

"You say it's a paradise," she replies. "That's good enough for me."

You can hardly argue with that.

The End

Dr. Vivaldi steadies the *Allegro* on a northwest course. Then you take the helm while Pete and Maiko trim the sails.

As the hours pass, the wind freshens, and the *Allegro* flies through the blue-green seas. A wandering albatross swoops down to inspect the boat. You marvel at its enormous wingspan as it circles you and then glides downwind just above the waves.

Eric climbs up from the cabin. He is looking a lot better. He checks the compass heading. "You've become quite a sailor," he says. "We're just about on course for Katar Atoll, a beautiful ring of coral reefs. If the wind holds, we should be there by nightfall."

"Smoke on the horizon dead ahead. It's an island!" Pete shouts. He squints through the binoculars. "It's a volcano!"

"There's no island shown on the chart," says Eric.

"Then this is it—the new island!" Dr. Vivaldi observes.

Maiko grabs the binoculars out of Pete's hands. "That island will be worth a billion dollars someday," he says.

"Look! Waves coming!" Pete points to a line of twenty-foot swells rolling toward the *Allegro*.

"Bring 'er thirty degrees to starboard," Eric orders. "Trim the sails. We'll take the waves just off the port bow."

Turn to page 26.

The ship rides easily through the waves, which are small compared to the tidal wave you rode out earlier.

"These waves are caused by a minor earthquake on the island," Dr. Vivaldi says.

"It could have been a lot worse," Eric says.

Dr. Vivaldi agrees. "The next one may be."

Maiko is standing on the deckhouse, holding on to the mast for balance. "Have you thought of this, mates?" he says. "That island has never been there before. It doesn't belong to any country. The first people to get there will own it. We could start our own country, make our own laws, run it any way we like."

"It might not be wise to think along those lines just yet," says Dr. Vivaldi. "If that volcano lets loose again while we're ashore, it could wipe us out before we elect you president, Maiko."

Eric laughs. "It's too late today, anyway." He points off to starboard. "We'll anchor off Katar Atoll for the night. Tomorrow we'll decide what to do."

Turn to page 30.

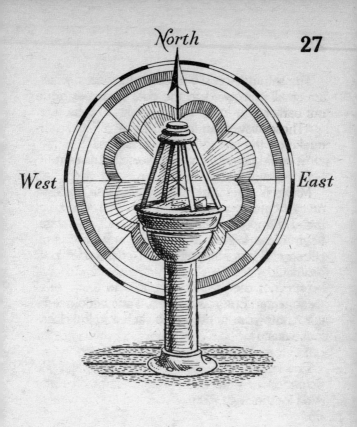

If you tell Dr. Vivaldi to steer north,
turn to page 7.

If you tell her to steer northwest,
turn to page 25.

If you tell her to steer northeast, east, or
southeast, turn to page 20.

If you tell her to steer south, southwest, or
west, turn to page 22.

28

You and Pete have been drifting in the life raft for five days now. Pete is curled up across from you, mumbling to himself. It looks as if he was hurt a lot worse than he let on.

All your water and most of the biscuits are gone. You are too thirsty to eat the rest. Your thirst increases by the hour.

Water! Water! Right now, nothing else matters. Your throat is burning. *Water. . . .*

You slump over the side of the raft and stare down at the trillions and trillions and trillions of gallons of water. Half the water in the world. The Pacific Ocean.

You know you're not supposed to drink salty ocean water. But you want to. Your body needs it. You cup your hand and lower it into the clear, cool water.

If you drink some ocean water, turn to page 54.

If you keep yourself from drinking the water, turn to page 33.

That night the crew takes turns standing watch. At midnight, it's your turn. While the others sleep, you sit alone on the foredeck, gazing at the new island silhouetted in the moonlight. Looking through the binoculars, you can make out a faint wisp of smoke rising from the mountaintop.

Suddenly, Maiko is standing next to you. He's holding a duffel bag in one hand and a spear gun in the other.

"Couldn't sleep?" you ask.

"I didn't want to sleep," he says. "I've been thinking about how I could own a whole country."

"What do you mean?"

"I'm taking the sailing skiff in to shore. I'm going to be the first man to stand on the new island. It's going to be *my* country!"

"But you can't take the skiff without Eric's permission."

"Oh, yes, I can, because I'm making the law on the new island."

"I'm going to wake the others," you say.

Maiko points his gun at you. "No, you're not, unless you want to be speared like a fat fish." His mouth twists into a crooked smile. "I wouldn't want to do that. You're a good sort. In fact, I want you to come along. I'll give you a share of the island. We'll be back on the *Allegro* by dawn, after I've planted my flag on shore."

If you want to go with Maiko, turn to page 37.

If you insist on staying on the Allegro, *turn to page 39.*

Before turning in for a little sleep, you stop at Eric's bunk. He seems very tired as he motions you toward him. "I can tell by the feel of the sea that we're in the path of a typhoon," he murmurs. "We may have to change course."

"To what?"

He shakes his head. "What's our heading right now?"

"We're heading east."

"Judging by the direction of the waves and the wind, the storm center is due east, and it's probably headed right at us. The right side of the storm is the dangerous side. Try to keep to the left of the storm path." Eric's eyes close, and he dozes off.

You hurry up to the deck. You must tell Dr. Vivaldi to change course. But which way should you tell her to turn?

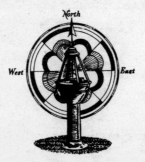

If you tell her to steer to the north,
turn to page 40.

If you tell her to steer to the west or the south,
turn to page 43.

You desperately want to **drink the salt water,** but you know that to do so **would be a sure** road to death.

You curl up in the raft and wait. Pete is asleep. You keep watch, hour after hour. At last you see something in the water. It's a boat! It seems to be dead in the water. You start paddling the raft toward it. Pete sits up, smiling for the first time since the tidal wave engulfed the *Allegro.*

You are too weak to paddle for long. Fortunately, the wind is blowing you toward the boat. You only have to paddle enough to make sure that you do not drift past it. Soon you can see its name painted on the bow—*Serena,* and below that, Honolulu. The bow is much higher than the stern, and waves are breaking over the rear deck.

"It's a wreck!" Pete cries.

"It must have gone aground on a reef," you say. "It looks like a fishing boat."

Go on to the next page.

Turn to page 36.

A half hour later the current brings you along-side the vessel, and you climb onto its slanting deck. The ship is in good condition, but there is no sign of the crew.

"They must have taken the lifeboat and tried to find land," Pete figures.

You scramble up the deck to the main cabin and climb through the hatch, past the bunks and chart table, then down a ladder into the hold. Pete follows close behind.

"Look, I've found a water tank." He points to a wooden barrel with a brass spigot. You find a row of mugs hanging on the wall, and you hold one under the spigot while Pete turns it on. A stream of water fills the mug, and the two of you eagerly quench your thirst.

Pete smiles at you and rubs his forehead. "Thank goodness they left this water!"

As he speaks, you pry the lid off the tank and look inside. "There are about four or five gallons left."

"We'll have to ration it," says Pete, "but this will keep us going for at least a week."

Feeling stronger, you search the boat for food. You find only a tin of dried apples and a bag of rice. You also find a tool kit, an alcohol stove, and a few packs of matches.

Turn to page 44.

This is the chance of a lifetime. You could be the first person to set foot on a new island. You could start a whole new country. "I'll go," you tell Maiko.

Maiko unties the sailing skiff and the two of you silently climb into it. Maiko lets the skiff drift downwind a bit before he raises the sails. The breeze has freshened, and the skiff flies through the gentle waves, riding the swells with ease. The new island grows larger and larger in the moonlight. Maiko rants about his new kingdom, the big hotels he will build, and how rich he will become. You begin to realize that he has become delirious with his visions of wealth and power. But your thoughts are interrupted by a rumbling from the shore. Could it be an earthquake? Is the volcano about to erupt?

"I think we'd better go back to the *Allegro*," you say.

Maiko spins around. Even in the pale light of the moon, you can see the gleam of madness in his eyes. "Not until I set foot on shore," he says, "and claim this island as my own!"

Maiko's spear gun is lying in the bilge. Using it may be your only hope against this madman.

If you try to grab the spear gun and demand he take you back to the Allegro, *turn to page 50.*

If you bide your time, turn to page 55.

"I'm staying here," you say.

"No," says Maiko. "I can't let you stay. It will interfere with my plans." He lifts his spear gun and motions you into the skiff. Then he grabs an inflatable life-raft pack, steps into the skiff, and casts it loose. He raises the sails, and the skiff rapidly sails away from the *Allegro*. You want to yell for the others, but there is little doubt that Maiko would use his gun on you. He seems to have gone mad. Your only choice is to play along with his crazy scheme.

Maiko abruptly heads the boat into the wind, and it lies motionless in the water, sails flapping. "OK, this is where you get out," he says.

"What do you mean?"

"Don't worry. I'm giving you your own boat." He unrolls the rubber raft and pulls the pin that inflates it with carbon dioxide. Then he throws it over the side.

"Get in," he orders.

You jump into the raft. Maiko tosses you a canteen of water.

"Hey, there are no oars in this raft!"

"If I gave you oars, you might get back to the *Allegro*," he says. "Instead, the wind will blow you out to sea." Maiko casts off your raft. His sails catch the wind and the skiff leaps away.

"Come back!" you yell. "I can't last long in this raft!"

"You're a clever sailor," Maiko yells back. "You'll get along OK."

You yell for a while longer, until you realize it won't help.

Turn to page 71.

40

You tell Dr. Vivaldi to steer north. Then you go below for some badly needed rest.

Hours later, you awaken to the rolling and pitching of the boat as it is knocked about by wild waves. The wind sounds like the roar of a jet plane. You can barely hear Maiko yell, *"It's your turn to take the wheel!"*

Wearily, you put on your slicker and climb up onto the deck.

Even in the darkness you can see that the ocean is white with foam and spray. You work your way back to the wheel and sit down next to Dr. Vivaldi. "I'm done in," she shouts over the wind. "You'll have to take over."

You look at the sails. They've been ripped to shreds. Their tattered remnants flap wildly in the wind.

Dr. Vivaldi rests a hand on your shoulder. Her voice is tense. "I've never sailed in weather this bad."

You do your best to steer the boat. The waves smash so hard against the hull that you're afraid it will break up. At times the boat careens down a long, steep wave and you fear that the bow will knife down and carry you all to the bottom.

Go on to page 42.

You try to remember everything you've ever learned about heavy-weather sailing.

Maiko staggers up on deck. "This storm will kill us!" he cries. "We've got to do something."

If you tell him to set the small heavy-weather sail in order to try and steady the boat, turn to page 58.

If you decide that even the heavy-weather sail might put too much strain on the boat, turn to page 59.

If you decide to go to the stern and trail heavy ropes in order to slow the boat and stabilize it, turn to page 64.

You've decided that by setting a course either to the south or the west you will be able to keep the *Allegro* on the safe side of the storm.

But, of those two, which is the better one to follow? You take a look at the chart.

If you set course to the west, turn to page 112.

If you set course to the south, turn to page 63.

44

The day is almost over. You and Pete climb up to the *Serena*'s foredeck and nibble on a dried apple as you watch the sun dip below the horizon.

"What now?" Pete asks.

"We need more food," you answer. "Tomorrow we must catch some fish."

The next morning you are up early. Using a knife you have found in the tool kit, you fashion a crude spear. You wonder whether it would be foolish to go over the side. You've seen a couple of barracuda lurking nearby.

If you dive over the side, go on to page 45.

If you decide to wait, turn to page 49.

You get your spear ready. Pete stands beside you at the rail. "I don't see any barracuda now," he says.

You peer into the water and spot three fat sunfish. You dive over the side and head straight down. You strike at the closest one. It darts away. It swims closer and you strike again. It swims away easily. You surface for air and then dive again. The sunfish glides by. You stab at it with your spear, and this time you get it.

As you start toward the boat with your catch, a long, dark shape comes toward you. *It's a barracuda!* You shoot to the surface and Pete pulls you aboard. The sun above you is hot, but you begin to shiver. There, on your spear, is your first catch. That evening you and Pete have a feast of rice and fish.

During the next week you become much better at spearing fish. The barracuda give you a few anxious moments, but after a while you almost feel used to them. Now that you have food, Pete seems to be healing rapidly. You spend your days swimming and exploring the reef. Soon you have a collection of beautiful seashells. One large blue one is like no shell you've ever seen.

Go on to the next page.

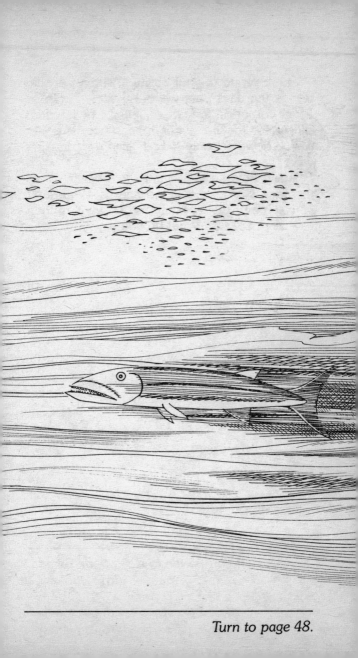

Turn to page 48.

You're proud of your ability to survive at sea. Yet, as the days pass without a sign of ship or plane, you begin to fear you'll never be rescued. Except for the fish, your food supply is gone. You're down to only a half gallon of drinking water.

Finally Pete says, "I can't stand waiting here anymore. No one's going to find us. Why don't we catch and dry as many fish as we can, then take off in the raft. What do you say?"

If you decide to stay on the Serena, *turn to page 53.*

If you decide to set out in the raft, turn to page 80.

You and Pete decide that you are not desperate enough to dive in near the barracuda. You wait and watch, hoping a ship or plane will spot you.

"Suppose a ship does pass nearby?" asks Pete. "What makes you think they would see a signal from us?"

"I don't know," you reply.

Another day passes. Your eyes hurt from staring out to sea for so long. You are lying in your bunk resting when you hear Pete calling. *"A ship! Look!"*

You race up the ladder and look where Pete is pointing. It's a freighter, maybe five or six miles away. At that distance there is no use waving or yelling. The two of you stare helplessly, not daring to hope that the ship will turn toward you.

Then your heart sinks. "It's passing us by. I don't think its course will bring it any closer than it is right now. If only we could signal them!"

"There's one way to do it," says Pete.

"What?"

"Set this ship on fire."

You look at Pete to see if he is joking, but his expression is serious.

"We'd have to get back in the raft," you say.

He nods. "I know. It's an awful risk to take, but I can't stand waiting another minute. I'm willing to risk it, if you are."

You gaze out again at the distant ship.

If you decide to set the Serena *on fire, turn to page 109.*

If not, turn to page 106.

You grab the spear gun. As you close your
fingers around the handle, Maiko lunges for you.
The boat rocks wildly. You try to get your balance, but Maiko's heavy hand clamps down on
your wrist. He wrestles the gun out of your hand.

"So, I have a traitor on my hands. When we
reach shore, you will be hanged."

"You can't do that!" you cry.

"I can do anything I want in *Maikoland*!" he
yells. "This new island is *my* country!"

For the next hour you sit, rubbing your bruised
wrist, wondering if you could ever escape. Mean-
while, the sky is growing pink and orange in the
east. In the west, the sea is about to devour the

fading moon. The island looms larger. You're almost there.

"Ah, I see a good spot to land." Maiko points to a cove protected from the breakers.

He lets out the sail and steers the boat between two enormous boulders that jut into the ocean. The sky is light now, and you can see the island clearly. Maiko heads the skiff toward the barren, gray beach of volcanic ash and pitted rocks.

Go on to page 52.

52

"No one could live on this island," you say. "It's a wasteland."

"You are a fool as well as a traitor," Maiko says. "Volcanic soil is very fertile. In a few years this shore will be lined with palm trees."

In a moment the skiff is aground. Maiko leaps out and jumps up and down in the fine gray sand. *"It's mine! It's mine!"* he shouts. *"A new country and it's all mine!"*

But even as he is yelling, you see a burst of flame and smoke rising from the volcano.

If you run to take shelter under an overhanging rock, turn to page 67.

If you push the skiff off the beach and shield your head with your arms as best you can, turn to page 75.

You and Pete decide not to risk taking the raft out to sea. Early the next morning, you are sitting on top of the cabin house, hoping, as always, to see a ship on the horizon. This time, you do see something. A small vessel is headed straight at you! You shout to Pete, and a moment later he joins you on deck. You both cheer and jump for joy.

"It looks like a Coast Guard ship," says Pete.

As the boat gets closer, you shout and wave. Sailors on deck wave back. Soon the boat comes alongside. You greet the sailors with hugs and cheers.

"We had no idea anyone was here," says the captain, as you climb aboard his ship. "The crew of the *Serena* made it to Etuk in their lifeboat, and we came to see if we could pull their trawler off the reef and tow it back to port."

The captain holds a memorial service for your lost crewmates. You'll never forget their friendship.

A few days later you and Pete are on a 767 jet, flying home. You don't know it yet (though you'll soon find out), but in your duffel bag is one of the rarest and most valuable seashells in the world.

The End

The water tastes cool. You gulp first one handful and then another. Soon you feel worse than ever, and thirstier than you could imagine possible. You splash the cool water on your face, but it doesn't help. You're burning up inside.

Pete stirs. "How are you?" he asks.

You try to answer, but your throat is too parched to utter a word. Half conscious now, you listen to the sloshing of the waves as the sun sinks lower in the west.

"A ship! A ship!" Pete is shaking you. But you are too weak to answer him. The sea has already claimed three of the *Allegro*'s crew. You will be the fourth.

Your last thought in life is that Pete, at least, will be rescued.

The End

You decide to play along with Maiko until you have a better chance to overpower him. "It's exciting to think that you will be king of a whole new country," you say.

Maiko turns toward you. "Yes, it is, yes!" His eyes are wild with greed.

You watch as Maiko trims the sails. Then your eyes fasten on the wisps of smoke curling up from the volcano's cone. You hear the distant rumble of thunder. The wind increases, and the skiff heels at an angle as it cuts through the waves. The air smells faintly of sulphur.

"Look at the smoke now," you say. "The volcano is going to blow its top. Please turn back!"

"Never!" Maiko shouts. His eyes are fixed on the island like a thirsty desert traveler staring at an oasis. He seems to be in a trance.

Now is your chance! You grab the spear gun. "We're turning around," you say as you point the gun at him.

"You little rat!" Maiko starts toward you, but the gun, designed to pierce the heart of an 800-pound shark, is steady in your hand. Even in his mad state, Maiko can tell you mean business.

He slumps back. "All right," he says, "but I will never forget this. Someday you will regret that you kept me from my island, my kingdom!"

Your eyes never leave Maiko as you swing the boat around and head back toward the *Allegro*. "Trim the sails!" you order.

Turn to page 57.

Within an hour, daylight is upon you. You strain your eyes to see the *Allegro*. Finally you see it, but your heart skips a beat. The *Allegro* is under way—sailing away from you. You will never catch up in the skiff. Why are they deserting you?

"Look!" Maiko points toward the island. Jets of flame and debris are spewing from the cone of the volcano. A huge plume of smoke billows forth, enshrouding the whole island.

"It's blowing!" Maiko shouts.

Turn to page 68.

"Set the storm trysail!" you shout, trying to be heard over the shrieking wind.

You can tell that Maiko is scared. Otherwise, he would never work so hard. Still, it takes ten minutes for him to raise the heavy canvas sail. Every minute or so he stops and clings to the boom as huge waves break over the boat.

Once the sail is set, the *Allegro* comes to life and surges through the water. Now the sloop has the power it needs to work through the monstrous waves.

Hour after hour, you steer the boat blindly through the gale, until you feel drained of every ounce of strength. But you stay with it. The worst part of the storm is over. Then Eric is at your side. "I'm feeling better!" he shouts over the wind, "and you . . . you saved us. You are a real sailor."

He takes hold of the wheel. You go below deck and collapse, exhausted, in your bunk. Already the wind and waves seem to be easing. You feel a rare sense of happiness. You have battled the raging seas—and won.

The End

You decide that the wind is too much even for the heavy-weather sail. You snap on your safety belt and check to make sure it will hold. Then you grab the wheel firmly, gritting your teeth as your ordeal begins.

Wave after wave batters the *Allegro*. You have to fight the wheel to keep the boat from going broadside.

Your strength is giving out. If only Eric were able to take the helm! You want to get Maiko to take over again, but he has gone below deck, and the hatch is closed. You can't leave the wheel. You want to scream. But in this wind, no one would hear you.

Then you see it—a freak wave twice as high as anything yet. The top is curling over. It's going to break over the boat. You hold on to the wheel with all your strength as the monster wave heaves the *Allegro* on its side. You are underwater, then under the boat itself! Your lungs are about to burst.

Slowly, the *Allegro* rights itself. But you're drifting away.

Turn to page 60.

Go on to page 62.

62

Another wave lifts you up and carries you against the lifelines. You grab hold and pull yourself back on deck. You are safe for the moment. But the *Allegro* is a wreck. The mast and boom have broken off. The deck is littered with line and ropes, split wood and bent metal.

The hatch opens. Dr. Vivaldi looks out. "I never thought we'd see you again. Are you all right? The boat's half full of water, but it's a little better in the cabin."

Gratefully, you stumble into the cabin. Water sloshes against your legs, Eric is sitting up in his bunk, rubbing his head. "What a boat! We flipped over and we're still afloat. What a sailor you are!"

You smile weakly at the compliment, for you have almost no strength left.

Turn to page 66.

You set the *Allegro* on a course to the south. Then you and Pete troll for fish while Dr. Vivaldi steers the boat. The *Allegro* sails briskly along in the breeze. Before turning in for the night, you sit on the foredeck and look out at the waves shimmering in the moonlight.

You sleep soundly and are awakened by a loud cry. *"Land ho!"* You eagerly climb up on deck and join the others gazing out at the familiar sight up ahead.

Dr. Vivaldi looks at you, shaking her head. "Your course took us back to Bariba Island! Did you think we'd find the Arkasaur *here*?"

Only then do you realize that if you had studied the chart more closely, you wouldn't have set a course to the south.

"Well, that's OK," says Eric. "We need a week's rest and fresh supplies."

"Yes," says Dr. Vivaldi. "I think next time our luck will change and we'll find the Arkasaur."

"Here's to our next trip!" says Pete.

You cheer along with the others, though you feel a little sad. School starts in a couple of weeks, and you won't be on the next trip.

The End

You've heard that towing warps—heavy ropes—will help slow a boat and stabilize it in violent seas.

You ask Maiko to take the wheel, and you get a coil of heavy line out of the stern locker. Then you inch your way along the heaving, slippery deck, dragging one end of the rope with you to the stern. You are hitching it to the after cleat when you hear Maiko scream. "WATCH OUT!"

A freak wave, coming from the port quarter, hits you like a flying waterfall. It sweeps you straightaway into the sea.

"Help!" you cry, but you know that help won't come. There's no way the *Allegro* can turn around in a sea like this.

You see the boat one more time, as Maiko waves helplessly at you, before the next wave carries you under.

The End

The wind and waves diminish. The fury of the storm has passed. The *Allegro* drifts helplessly in the water. At last, the sun breaks through the clouds. The wind becomes a gentle breeze. Early the next morning you are rescued by a passing freighter.

You never did find the Arkasaur, but you sailed through one of the worst typhoons of the year, and you survived.

The End

You run across the fine, dusty sand, headed for the shelter of the big rock. If you can get there before the blast hits, you might have a chance.

But the sand is so powdery that with each step you sink in up to your ankles. It's like trying to run through deep, soft snow. You haven't quite reached shelter before the fiery blast strikes you down.

The End

"Quick, lower the sails," you cry. Maiko unties the halyard as you head the boat into the wind. The sail and boom come crashing down.

"Duck!" But your words are drowned out by the thunderous noise of the blowout. You cringe as a hurricane wind strikes the boat with a fury that takes your breath away. The wind rocks the boat wildly, driving it through the waves.

How long this terror lasts, you can't guess. Finally the wind subsides.

"Maiko!" you yell.

There is no answer. You sit upright. Maiko is gone. You cast your eyes around the choppy sea. Short, high waves are traveling every which way. It's hard to see very far, and there is no sign of Maiko.

The island is partly obscured by smoke and haze, but you can see red-hot lava glowing on the volcano.

You are alone in the skiff. You have a jug of drinking water and a day's supply of rations, but you are far from land, except for the new island, which by now may be covered with hot flowing lava. What should you do?

If you decide to try to sail to Etuk, the nearest inhabited island, 200 miles to the west, turn to page 74.

If you decide to stay within sight of the new island, in hopes that you will be rescued, turn to page 77.

If you decide to try to find a safe landing place on the new island, turn to page 78.

If you decide to wait for the voyage to begin on the next island, turn to page 78.

Two days have passed. You are still alone, drifting in your tiny raft in the middle of the Pacific Ocean. There's been no sign of a plane or ship. Even the birds and flying fish have deserted you.

You feel desperate and afraid, but you are grateful that you didn't continue on to the island with Maiko. Only a few hours after he set you adrift, a fiery explosion lit the sky. The volcano let loose such heat and light that, even far out at sea, you felt the flush of heat on your face. The sudden wind sent your raft skidding over the water and left you rocking in a confusion of waves.

Threatening clouds have obscured the sun so you can't even tell which way you've been drifting. There have been a couple of rain-showers, and you've been able to cup your hands and catch a little water.

As the day passes you feel weaker and weaker. You lie in the raft, head propped on a life jacket. You try to stop yourself, but you begin to cry. You've never felt so lonely.

Maybe the best thing to do is to accept your fate: just lie there, close your eyes, and wait for the end to come. It would be easier that way.

If you close your eyes and give up all hope, turn to page 79.

If you refuse to give up hope, turn to page 113.

You awaken to find yourself lying in a bunk. By the motion of the boat and sound of the engine, you can tell that you are on a motor yacht. Who has rescued you?

You sit up and peer through the porthole. The new island is only a couple of miles away. The volcano top was knocked off by that last eruption. Now only a thin wisp of smoke drifts downwind from the crater.

"So, you are awake!"

You turn, startled, to see a man wearing a white jacket over a red shirt standing next to your bunk.

"Thank you for saving my life," you say. "Who are you?"

"My name is Jason Lucus, and it is enough for you to know that I am a businessman. You don't need to tell me who you are. We have made radio contact with the *Allegro*. We are heading toward her. In less than two hours you will be safely back with your friends."

You start to thank him, but he holds up his hand. "First, I want you to sign this paper."

"Why? What does it say?" you demand.

"It says that we will pay you $10,000 for any claim you might have to the new island. We were watching you through binoculars. You were the first person to stand on the island. You might succeed in claiming it as your property."

If you sign the paper, turn to page 82.

If you refuse, turn to page 84.

You push the skiff off the beach and jump in, covering your head with your arms.

"Where do you think you're going?" Maiko screams, but his voice is drowned out by the roar and the blast of superheated air that blows your skiff like a shot out of the cove. As you lie face down, holding your breath, the back of your neck is singed by the hot wind.

Just as suddenly, the wind dies. The boat rocks wildly. You can breathe a little now, but you feel just barely alive. A moment later you lose consciousness.

Turn to page 72.

Deciding to stay within sight of the island you sail back and forth, keeping a few miles offshore. You want to be near enough to the island to be spotted by any plane flying in to investigate the volcano, but not so close as to risk being wiped out if the mountain should blow.

Several hours later you hear a sound overhead. Jets. Navy fighters! They swoop low. They're dipping their wings. They see you!

Within hours you are rescued by a helicopter from the aircraft carrier *Ranger*. The pilot tells you that the *Allegro* is safe, and that you will soon be reunited with your friends.

"Who will own the new island?" you ask the helicopter pilot.

"Well," he says, "I hear that if it doesn't blow its top and sink into the sea, the United Nations will own it. It may be years before it's safe to build anything there. In the meantime, scientists from all over the world will come here to study it."

"I like that idea," you say, as you stand on the deck, looking out over the azure blue sea.

The End

There's some risk in landing on the island, but there are risks in staying at sea, too. Besides, you'd love to be the first person to set foot on a brand-new island.

The sun has just sunk behind the peak of the volcano when your skiff glides through the waves and onto the beach.

Could it be true? *You* own a whole island? And could you be its ruler? But what an island it is. It looks more like an alien planet. There is no trace of life, only gray rocks and gray sand and ash. The thick smell of sulphur hangs in the air. An island newly born, yet dead.

You start up the rough mountain slope. From the ridge above you'll have a better view. You notice a small pond. There are lots of fish swimming in it. They must have been deposited by the tidal wave. You'll be able to catch enough fish to live on. When it rains you will have water from hollows in the rocks. The weather is warm enough so that with fish to eat, water to drink, and overhanging rocks for shelter, you'll be able to survive for awhile. Search planes are sure to pass over the island. You feel certain you will be rescued.

As you wait, you wonder what rights you will have to the new island. As the first human being to discover it and live on it, will you really be declared its owner? Or will your country be the owner? Or will it be like Antarctica, which is owned by no country?

Maybe the island will be named after you. At the very least you'll be famous.

The End

You close your eyes and try to sleep. You don't want to look ever again at the endless panorama of waves and sky. You have given up all hope of rescue. You know you will never see another human being again.

Soon it will be over.

The End

80

You and Pete fashion a small sail from a tarpaulin you find on the *Serena*. You pack aboard your drinking water and a supply of dried fish, take a last look at the *Serena*, and push off. A stiff wind quickly carries you away from the wreck.

You've been adrift most of the day when you spot a fishing boat about a mile and a half to the north. You can tell from the sun that it's headed southeast, possibly bound for Bariba. If only you could signal it, but it's too far away. You're going to have to catch it, or at least come pretty close.

"How fast do you think it's going?" you ask Pete.

He squints at the horizon. "I don't know why," he says, "but I'd say only about five knots. Still, that's twice as fast as this raft."

At this point only two courses make any sense at all: north and northeast. Which way should you steer?

If you decide to head north, turn to page 96.

*If you decide to sail northeast,
turn to page 118.*

You sign the paper, and Lucus hands you a stack of $100 bills. You ruffle through them.

"You're a smart kid," Lucus says.

Soon you are safely back on board the *Allegro*, with $10,000 in your pocket. You tell your friends about your adventure. Eric shakes his head as you tell him how Maiko got you to take the skiff over to the new island. You gaze out at it now, just a few miles across the water. Its gray mountainous slopes have taken on a pink hue in the late afternoon sun. A thin plume of white smoke rises from the top of the volcano. You wonder whether you were wise to sell your claim to it for only $10,000.

Suddenly there is a bright red flash on the eastern horizon. It is quickly followed by a billowing plume of smoke, then a roar that sounds like a thousand cannons. You cover your ears. Then you cringe as a shock wave heels the *Allegro* sharply over on its side. But the boat quickly rights itself, and the wind subsides almost as quickly as it had risen.

You all stare toward the island, but all you can see in the distance is a thick gray haze.

"We've seen millions of years of earth history in a few days," says Pete.

"Now we can resume our search for the Arkasaur," Dr. Vivaldi observes.

You're eager to help find the Arkasaur, but right now you can't stop thinking about what you'll do with the $10,000.

The End

84

You look Jason Lucus in the eye. "If I have a right to that island, I don't want to sell it for $10,000. It must be worth a lot more than that!"

Lucus's face reddens, and his lips tighten into a thin white line. "I am a generous man, but I never make the same offer twice!"

He draws a silver pistol from the inside pocket of his white linen jacket.

"You should understand," he continues in his cold voice, "I really didn't want to kill you. In fact, I was willing to pay $10,000 to *avoid* killing you. But that wasn't enough for you. GET UP ON DECK!"

You start up the ladder, with the blunt muzzle of his revolver pressing between your shoulder blades.

"Are you going to shoot me?"

A cruel laugh escapes from Lucus's mouth. "I can't bear the sight of blood. That's why I prefer to have you lose your balance and fall overboard."

As you step up on deck, Lucus twists you around. With one swift movement he lifts you over his shoulders and hurls you over the rail.

Turn to page 86.

Screaming, you hit the water. Looking up, you see a sailor watching you from the stern of the yacht. He unhooks a Styrofoam life buoy and throws it toward you. "Sorry I can't do more," he calls, "but they'd have my skin next."

The yacht accelerates, leaving you to struggle in its foamy white wake.

You swim to the buoy. It's shaped like a U and is big enough to climb on top.

For the moment you are safe. There is no land in sight. But soon your spirits are lifted. There is a waterproof bag attached to the buoy. You open it, taking care to keep the contents dry, and find a half-gallon plastic bottle of fresh water, three squares of chocolate wrapped in foil, two packs of matches, and two rocket flares.

The sun is setting. Darkness comes quickly in the tropics, and soon you have a thousand stars for company. The sea is calm, the air warm. You're going to make it through the night, but you are lonely and, to tell the truth, scared.

If you send up one of the rocket flares, turn to page 95.

If you decide to save them until you see the lights of a ship, turn to page 116.

You sail north, toward the cloud, but as the hours go by, it hardly seems closer. You wonder whether you are chasing a mirage.

Then, as the sun sinks in the west, you make out a shape under the cloud. It is a mountain, one you've seen before. It is the volcano on the new island! You've been sailing in a circle, and you have come back to the same place you started.

With neither the strength nor the will to make it to Etuk, you stay on course for the new island. Surely the Navy will be investigating. Scientists will want to study it. Maybe a plane will spot you. You sail on desperately as darkness overtakes you.

The stars appear, but they quickly vanish, and the night turns pitch black. The air is hot. You lie exhausted in the skiff and sleep a fretful sleep. You dream of mountains of lava flowing down the mountainside, ever about to engulf you as you run, run, run, run from the bubbling red tide. . . .

Turn to page 97.

You hitch your rope around the neck of the Arkasaur. The creature takes off through the water at tremendous speed, leaving a huge wake behind it. Looking down, you can see its gigantic flippers paddling the water behind you with the force of a thousand oars. The speed causes the beast to rise high in the water. It's like riding a hydrofoil!

Turn to page 90.

If the creature were to dive, your raft would surely capsize, and you might be sucked down into a whirlpool. There is nothing you can do but trust fate. You lie in the raft, straddling the Arkasaur's back as if you were riding a horse or a whale. It's the ride of your life!

Hour after hour you fly over the waves. When darkness falls, you relax, close your eyes, and sleep. Later you are violently awakened. You're underwater—caught in a whirling current that flips you wildly over and over. *Smash!* Your hand strikes hard sand. Your neck twists as a surging wave whips you over. You struggle upward. Sunlight is streaming through. You reach the surface and gasp as another wave lashes you. This time your legs hit bottom. Your lungs scream for air. Then another wave hurls you against the beach. You struggle out of the surf and flop on dry, warm sand. You feel yourself drifting into unconsciousness, but not before you see a blurred, watery vision of palm trees and thatched huts, and people running toward you.

Turn to page 99.

Hoping that Etuk still lies to the west, you sail in that direction. The breeze is fair and your hopes are high. But by nightfall you have seen no land, and not even a solitary bird. You set your tiller and sail as best you can, hoping the skiff will keep on course through the night.

You can't get comfortable lying in the skiff, and you sleep fitfully. Sometime during the night you are awakened by thunder. The sail has come loose in the wind. The boat is rocking and pitching in the choppy sea. Lightning flashes across the sky, revealing a swiftly moving line of jet black clouds. The water beneath is foamy white. You feel a chill wind increasing in force. It's a line squall that hits like a hurricane.

Like the stroke of a giant hand, the gale flips your little skiff over on its side. You hang on tightly, but you know it's all over. You are a sailor who, like many others before you, will perish in the wild and stormy sea.

The End

You're afraid that if you hitched on to the Arkasaur and it suddenly dove under the waves, you would be sucked down with it into the depths of the sea. You paddle away, hoping to get to a safe distance in case the creature dives or thrashes its giant body. You keep your eye on it while it whirls its long, powerful neck around to look at you. Suddenly it slips beneath the waves.

Go on to the next page.

You drift helplessly in the raft for the rest of the day and through the night. But, early the next morning, a passing freighter plucks you out of the water. You are barely alive and hardly able to swallow the fresh water and lemonade the crewmen pour into your mouth. It's two days more before you are able to sit up and tell the captain about your adventures. You can hardly blame him when he chuckles upon hearing of your encounter with the Arkasaur.

"An old sailor like me hears a pack of wild stories in a lifetime at sea," he says. He leans closer, and his weathered face crinkles as he smiles. "But the wildest ones come from poor wretches like you, dying of thirst and poisoned by too much salt and sun. It's then that the mind plays its strangest tricks. I know you believe that your story is true, but, let me tell you, you'll never see the Arkasaur when you're safe on the deck of a sound ship sailing in a fair breeze."

The captain has a kind face, and he speaks so sincerely that you begin to think your encounter with the Arkasaur was nothing but a dream.

The End

You've been unconscious, but now you're slowly coming to. There is ocean everywhere you look, but you are high above the waves, looking down through the windows of a helicopter.

"Glad to see you're still with us!" The cheerful voice belongs to a sandy-haired man. "We're from the aircraft carrier *Ranger*," he says, "and we'll be setting you down in about ten minutes."

"Thanks for picking me up. Have you seen a boat named the *Allegro*?"

"Yes, they asked us to try to locate you. They're sailing back to Bariba. We'll have you there by nightfall."

"I guess they didn't find the Arkasaur," you say.

"Not this time," the officer replies. "But I hope you'll keep looking. It's out there. I know it."

And so do you.

The End

You send up a rocket flare. Its red flame lights up the sky.

If there are any boats within twenty miles, surely they will see your rocket. Your eyes follow the horizon in a full circle as you strain to catch a glimpse of a light or a shape—anything. In the fading white light you do see something. A dark hump is rising from the water. It must be a small atoll, a coral reef, a mile or so away.

Whatever you were looking at fades into the darkness. But there's a bright star, a few degrees above the horizon, almost exactly above the object.

You start paddling toward the star. But will you ever reach it? Should you use all your strength to paddle, or should you save your strength and wait for the light of a passing ship?

If you paddle toward the star, turn to page 105.

If you save your strength, turn to page 107.

You steer north, but after fifteen or twenty minutes, you can see that you're not getting any closer to the fishing boat. You adjust your course, but the boat keeps moving away from you.

"We'll never catch it," says Pete.

You nod sadly as you scan the horizon, hoping to spot another boat. But there are none in sight. Nor do you see anything during the rest of the day, or the next, or the next. . . .

As the days go by, you grow weaker and weaker, until you realize that the fishing boat was your last hope for survival.

The End

You are awakened by a crash. Your skiff has drifted ashore. You jump out and pull the skiff up onto the dusty shore. You are on the new island. Maybe you are the first person to set foot here, but all that means is that you are the *only* person here. You are too weak and exhausted to do anything but lie in the beached skiff and wait.

The hours pass. You hear a faint rumbling. Looking up, you see one plane and then another. One plane swoops low and dips its wings. They've seen you! A rescue helicopter should reach you within hours. As long as the volcano holds off, you're as good as rescued.

The End

You awaken to find yourself lying on a cot in a thatched-roof house. A woman is standing over you. She smiles and hands you a mug. You drink eagerly. It's fresh, cool pineapple juice—the best you have ever tasted.

The woman tells you that you are on the island of Bori Rama, a tiny atoll 250 miles east of Bariba. Some fishermen found you washed up on the beach.

Go on to page 100.

Within the hour, you reach Eric on the radio telephone.

"I can't believe it's you!" he says. "There's no way your raft could have drifted all the way from the new island to Bori Rama in such a short time."

"It didn't drift," you say, and you explain your amazing ride with the Arkasaur.

"I really can't believe it," he says, "but I guess I have to, since it's the only way you could have traveled 400 miles in just ten hours. No ship or boat could travel that fast, and no planes or helicopters have landed on Bori Rama." He pauses a moment. "Hold on. Dr. Vivaldi wants to talk to you."

"Are we glad to hear from *you!*" she says.

"It's good to hear your voice," you tell her.

"I will want to hear all about your encounter with the Arkasaur," she says. "Now I'm more curious than ever about this fantastic animal. Are you willing to continue the search with us?"

"I'd sure like to, but I have to be at school in a couple of weeks."

"I'm sure I can arrange for you to miss a few weeks of school," she replies, "because you're going to learn a lot—and so will I—on the next voyage of the *Allegro.*"

The End

Looking up, you marvel at the coral dome over your head. It is so delicate that sunlight filters through. You climb onto a reef and gaze about in the eerie pinkish-green light.

It is a rare and beautiful place, but this doesn't change the fact that you are marooned. You have only a little food and water left.

As you sit, staring into the blue-green water, a strange shape rises from the depths. A primitive head and long rubbery neck protrude from the surface. The Arkasaur!

Turn to page 102.

The creature waves its head. Suddenly it dives, disappearing as quickly as it came.

What an eerie experience. Are you dreaming? Are you going mad?

What's that sound overhead? It must be a plane!

Turn to page 104.

You dive into the water, swim out of the grotto and climb onto the reef. Looking up, you see that it's a helicopter overhead. You grab the remaining rocket from your bag, light it, and send it up. You cross your fingers for one very long minute. Finally the light glows. Almost at once the chopper turns and swoops toward you. You see the American flag and the white star painted on the aircraft, and, as it settles in, seeking out a landing place on your tiny reef, the stenciled letters *U.S. NAVY*.

In a few minutes you're safely aboard the helicopter. The Navy pilots are amused when you tell them about your discovery. They just don't believe it. But you hardly care; you are so happy to learn from them that the *Allegro* reached Bariba safely.

By nightfall, you are reunited with the crew of the *Allegro*. Breathlessly, you tell everyone what happened.

"Do you think I was hallucinating?" you ask.

Dr. Vivaldi shakes her head. "No. Without a doubt you saw the Arkasaur."

"When do we set sail for the atoll?" asks Pete.

"I can chart our course," you add.

But Dr. Vivaldi stops you. "I've been giving this a lot of thought," she says. "The grotto is the Arkasaur's surface habitat. It is a miracle that this marvelous animal has survived for so long. We must be very careful not to upset the balance. It will have to be enough for us to know that the Arkasaur lives."

The End

You paddle toward the star. It's slow going but the wind helps you along. You wonder which way the current is running. It might carry you past the atoll without your realizing it.

Suddenly you hear the familiar sound of waves breaking. *Surf!* Then you see the coral atoll, silhouetted in the starlight. You paddle as hard as you can through the surf. A smoothly curving wave casts you up on the coral reef.

What a feeling to be back on land! You climb up on the beach and stretch out on the sand. You sip from your water bottle and munch on a square of chocolate as you watch the sun rise out of the sea.

Looking around, you see that the island is nothing more than a coral reef that curves around in a semicircle. It's less than half a mile across.

You walk down to the lagoon and dive into the clear blue water. Maybe you will catch a fish. You see a dark shape under the water. It looks like the entrance to a tunnel. You wonder where it could lead. Probably nowhere, but there is nothing else to do on this tiny island. You dive down and swim a few yards underwater and into the tunnel. You see light up ahead, so you swim on a little farther. When you come up, you're in a huge air bubble in an underwater cave. A grotto!

Turn to page 101.

The idea of burning your ship out from under you and getting back on the tiny raft is more than you can bear.

"If they don't come, we won't last long on that raft," you say. "At least we're safe here. And maybe we can think of some other way to signal a ship or plane."

Pete looks glum. "I'm not sure you're right," he says, "but . . ." His voice trails off, and you sit helplessly watching the freighter pass out of sight over the horizon.

As the days pass, your hopes fade. Your supplies and water are soon gone. No other ships or planes pass by. You and Pete grow weaker and weaker, until one day you know you just aren't going to make it.

That night you dream that a Coast Guard ship has anchored near the wreck of the *Serena*. The sailors on the ship launch a boat and row to the wreck. The wreck is deserted, except for two skeletons lying on the deck. You wake up in a cold sweat, certain that the dream will come true.

The End

You decide to save your strength, so you hang on to the life buoy and wait.

The hours pass. The stars swing around in the sky. Those in the west slip into the sea, while new ones rise in the east. There are no lights on the horizon now. You feel cold, even though the water seemed so warm. You doze off. When you open your eyes, there is a pink glow in the eastern sky. You've made it through the night.

You unwrap a chocolate bar and bite off a corner. When the sun comes up, you climb on top of your life buoy and get most of your body out of the water. In an hour or so you are warm again. Suddenly a stray wave breaks over the buoy and drenches you from head to toe.

An hour passes, and then another. You sip some water. You'll wait awhile before eating the last of your chocolate. The wind begins to freshen. Whitecaps form and waves smash into your tiny float.

Now you're really cold. You can't stop shivering. With trembling fingers, you eat another square of chocolate. It makes you feel queasy.

What's that noise overhead? A plane! Quickly you light the fuse of a rocket and hold the launcher. At the same time a wave hits you. Your pack and drinking water fly into the sea. But you hang on to the launcher, keeping the rocket pointed upward. In a moment, even in broad daylight, the bright red light of the rocket is visible high above you!

Turn to page 108.

108

This last effort has made you feel faint. You are slipping into unconsciousness.

Turn to page 94.

"Let's do it," you tell Pete. "I'll pile up everything that will burn, to make sure the whole boat catches fire. You load all our food and water aboard the raft."

As soon as Pete has the raft ready to cast off, you light the fire. You watch the flames leap and catch the old wooden timbers under the foredeck. Then you race to join Pete in the raft. He casts off and the two of you paddle until you're a safe distance away.

"I hope we did the right thing," he says.

You stare at the blazing hulk of the *Serena* and then at the ship on the horizon. Surely they must see the fire. Yet the ship continues on the same course, at the same speed.

"It's turning!" Pete cries.

"Are you sure?" Then you see that it *is* turning. You start to stand up and wave. The raft tilts dangerously and water spills in.

Turn to page 111.

"Sit down!" Pete laughs. "You'll sink us!"

An hour later all that's left of the *Serena* is some charred driftwood, but you and Pete are on the deck of the freighter *Valencia*, drinking cold soda and telling the captain about your adventure.

"That was pretty brave of you, setting that wreck afire," he says. "It's a lucky thing, too. There's a storm coming that would have carried the *Serena* right off the reef."

You're grateful to have survived, and sad about your friends who didn't.

The End

112

Once you have set the *Allegro* on its new course you go below for some sleep. You've never been so tired in your life, and you sleep a deep, dreamless sleep. Hours later you're awakened by excited voices on deck. The storm has passed, and the sun is already shining into the cabin.

You hurry up the ladder and find the others looking at a ring of cone-shaped peaks rising from the sea. "What a beautiful island," you say.

"Yes," Eric agrees. "It's Carina Island, the loveliest sight in all the Pacific. I've heard that sometimes sailors fall in love with this paradise and cannot bring themselves to leave it."

"Let's stay here a few days and rest," says Dr. Vivaldi.

Everyone agrees, and Eric sets the course. As the island draws closer, you find yourself hypnotized by the white sand beaches, the waving palms, and the scent of jasmine drifting to you from the shore.

"I have a feeling we aren't going to find the Arkasaur," says Eric.

"We may have found something equally wonderful," Dr. Vivaldi replies. "An enchanted island."

The End

You will never give up hope! You sit up and gaze in all directions at the endless sea. Tiny black spots dance before your eyes.

You dip one foot over the side of the raft. The water feels very warm, even for the tropics. Could this be the warm current that Dr. Vivaldi was telling you about? Could this be the habitat of the Arkasaur? At last you may have the chance to spot the most amazing creature on Earth. But what good will it do you, if you are going to die? You splash water on your face. It feels good, but salty. You never want to taste salt again.

Then you see it! First its lumpish gray-green head, then its rubbery, powerful neck rising ten feet or more above the waves. A hump rises out of the water behind it like a small island rising from the sea.

At that moment you should be more afraid than you've ever been, but you are actually more curious than frightened. Is this the one species of dinosaur that has survived for millions and millions of years? Could it be the first instance of an immortal animal?

Turn to page 115.

You have a coil of rope in your raft. The creature is coming closer. It could tip your raft over with a flick of one of its mighty flippers. But something about the creature gives you hope. It's not charging you like some hungry shark. Instead, it seems curious, too, like a higher form of mammal. Are you dreaming, or does it even seem *friendly*?

Now the creature is so close that you realize you could tie your raft onto its back fin and hitch a ride! That would be fun. Suppose, though, the creature turned on you, or suddenly dove under the waves.

If you try to hitch a ride on the Arkasaur, turn to page 89.

If not, turn to page 92.

You drift through the night. From time to time you doze off. Whenever you wake, you scan the horizon, hoping that you'll see a ship. But the only lights you see are phosphorescent streaks in the water.

Once again you doze off, but something awakens you. You peer over the edge. A dark white torpedo is coursing through the water. Its shape is unmistakable—a great white shark!

You cry out, but no one can hear you. No one can help.

The End

You steer northeast, hoping that your path will cross the path of the fishing boat. The wind picks up a bit, and the raft moves nicely along through the water. You keep your eyes fixed on your goal.

Very slowly the fishing boat grows larger. You're getting closer. You can see men on the deck. You wave. The boat changes course. It's heading right at you.

"Pete," you shout. "We're going to make it!"

The End

ABOUT THE AUTHOR

A graduate of Princeton University and Columbia Law School, EDWARD PACKARD lives in New York City, where he is a practicing lawyer. Mr. Packard conceived of the idea for the Choose Your Own Adventure® series in the course of telling stories to his children, Caroline, Andrea, and Wells.

ABOUT THE ILLUSTRATOR

PAUL GRANGER is a prize-winning illustrator and painter.